A Bread Basket for Grandma

Teaching Children Acceptance across all cultures
Embracing Kindness and Tolerance in our world

Written by: **Lori Tomenchok**
Illustrated by: **Marques Cannon**

Balboa Press books may be ordered through booksellers or by contacting:

Balboa Press
A Division of Hay House
1663 Liberty Drive
Bloomington, IN 47403
www.balboapress.com
844-682-1282

Because of the dynamic nature of the Internet, any web addresses or links contained in this book may have changed since publication and may no longer be valid. The views expressed in this work are solely those of the author and do not necessarily reflect the views of the publisher, and the publisher hereby disclaims any responsibility for them.

Any people depicted in stock imagery provided by Getty Images are models, and such images are being used for illustrative purposes only.
Certain stock imagery © Getty Images.

Interior Image Credit: Marques Cannon

ISBN: 978-1-9822-7129-9 (sc)
978-1-9822-7130-5 (e)

Library of Congress Control Number: 2021913378

Print information available on the last page.

Balboa Press rev. date: 07/22/2021

Dedication

This book is dedicated to my mom whose birthday fell on the day this story came to life as well as Pastor Jeff Bryan who sparked my inspiration to write this story.

It is also dedicated to every parent, grandparent, aunt, uncle, teacher, and person who has taken on the role to lovingly raise our children of future generations. As was once stated, it takes a village and it takes all of us to contribute to a world where love, peace and equality are the norm. It is my hope that this book will open the door to conversations about diversity and embracing differences. Please use this book as a starting point for teaching acceptance and in schools as a beginning to an anti-bias curriculum. On "heartwings" of love let this message fly throughout the world.

Preface

It was October 7, 2018. I was visiting my mom in South Carolina for her birthday. We woke up and had our usual morning coffee and were preparing to go to church. I grew up attending Sunday morning worship and did not expect anything unusual to happen that morning. We sat in our usual pew....2nd row on the left, Mom, then all the nieces and then me. The service started as usual with songs and prayers and then pastor Jeff called the children to the front for the children's message. He pulled out a basket of bread and began to speak. I had heard many children's stories and sermons. In fact, I had given a few myself in the 40 years of teaching and leading children in school, Sunday school, vacation bible school and more. The sermon was amazing, it expanded my heart. It made many of the little ones hungry for the bread, but it made me hungry to share the message with the world. We are positioned at a time in our world where expanding our hearts and minds is critical. As adults we need to learn to be tolerant, kind and accepting of all races, religions, and cultures. I have been an educator my entire life. I can say from experience that most young children share their love willingly and accept without reservation. I have taught in multicultural classrooms and my students love everyone, embracing them as a friend without question. If only we could remember to be as the little children, we might shift the tide and create a world where acceptance is the norm. Regardless of your race, culture, religious belief, and more, I urge you to Love your neighbor...

Pass it on.

Nalla jumped out of bed excited for the day ahead.

Not only was it International Day at School but it was Grandma B's birthday, and they were celebrating with a tea party after school!

Nalla chose her favorite outfit and shoes that Grandma bought her for her first day of school. She knew Grandma loved when she wore them! She quickly dressed and ran downstairs for breakfast.

Nalla ate her cereal while mom wrapped the bread they had baked the night before. Everyone in Nalla's class was bringing in bread from their family's ancestry.

Nalla baked **Chorag** which Grandma B made for all the holidays. She would watch Grandma carefully roll out the dough then braid it and make it into circles and twists. Sometimes Grandma would give her a ball of dough to create a shape of her own. They would brush it with egg and bake it. The house smelled delicious when the bread was done. Nalla could not wait to get to school to see all the breads the other children had made at home.

Nalla held her bread carefully on her lap while she rode to school. She thought about how exciting it would be to celebrate the faraway lands that she read about in story books and hear her friends tell stories about their grandparents traditions.

Nallas brother was in 6th grade. They were hanging maps in the hall to show where different people lived and where each bread originated from.

DIFFERENT LANDS

Nalla's teacher Miss Lori had decorated the classroom with pictures of different lands. There was a large basket on the table where they always sat for circle time. As each child came into the room Miss Lori placed their bread around the basket.

Nalla could hardly wait for class to begin.

Nalla played in the discovery center with her friends until the teacher cheerfully announced..." Good morning everyone, please join me at the carpet for circletime." The class gathered around Miss Lori chattering away as they settled on the carpet and began their International Day celebration.

Each child was given a turn to stand up and tell the class the story about their bread.

Nalla explained that her grandma was Assyrian and it was a family tradition to make **Chorag** for the holidays. She giggled as she realized her mom snuck some shortbread in the basket as well. That was Grandpa's favorite and he was from Scotland.

One by one her friends got up and talked about their families' bread. There was **Naan** from India, **Roti** from Pakistan, **Challah** from Israel, **Soda Bread** from Ireland, **Ciabatta** from Italy and others! There were many that she had never heard of or tasted such as Green Mealie bread, Nigerian Puff bread, Bannock (which she learned meant skann or scone), Po lo bao and more. As each story was told a piece of bread was placed in the basket. They were all different shapes, colors, and sizes!

When the children were finished with their stories, they exclaimed with delight at the beautiful basket their breads had created.

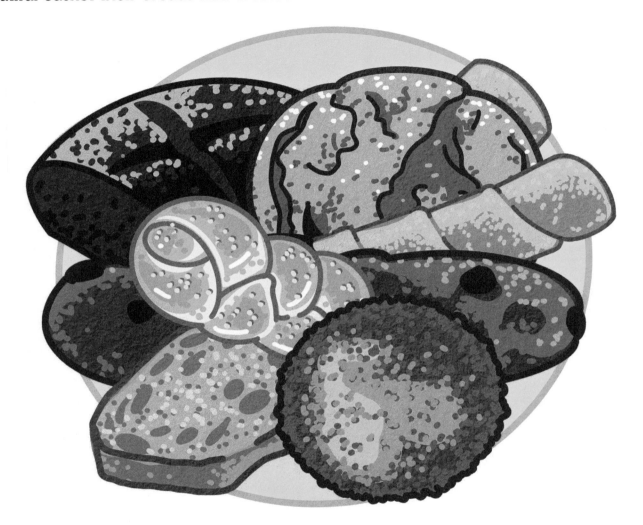

You know... Miss Lori Exclaimed.... this basket represents all of you! Look closely... each bread is unique. Not one bread is the same. There are different shapes, different colors and different sizes. They are each made in a different land. But they have one incredibly special thing in common. They are all bread! In this way they are all the SAME! We can love and enjoy each one for the tastes they have to offer.

This is just like all of you! Look around our circle. You are all unique. You come in different shapes, sizes, and colors. You each have families from different lands with different beliefs and traditions. But you share one special thing in common. **You are all people** and that **makes you all the same!!**

Nalla could feel her heart getting bigger and bigger. She looked around at all her friends. She loved them all the same. They were all looking around the circle smiling at each other with a love they knew they all shared.

They continued celebrating International Day tasting each other's delicious breads and treats.

They took a walk through the school to see the displays the other classes had placed in the hallways.

When the school day was over Nalla was given a basket of Bread as she lined up for the bus ride home. She could barely wait to get home. She knew Grandma would be waiting there to celebrate her birthday and Nalla knew what she wanted to do...

She jumped off the bus and ran up the porch steps. She knew it Grandma had the tea party all set up!

"Grandma, Grandma," Nalla exclaimed...
"look what I brought for you!"

Nalla held out her basket filled
with the delicious breads...

HAPPY BIRTHDAY GRANDMA!!

Grandma hugged Nalla close. They sat down at the tea party and shared tastes of the delicious breads adding some jellies and jams that grandma brought. Nalla excitedly told Grandma about her day. She especially liked what Miss Lori had said about everyone being the same.

As she shared this story with Grandma, she could sense that Grandma's heart was getting bigger and bigger too.

"You know Nalla" Grandma explained, "when we think a thought and add love from our heart maybe we can shift people's hearts. – Maybe the thoughts will grow wings and travel wherever we send it. We can send it to our friend next door or across the world, the universe and more! Maybe if we practice tolerance and kindness and send loving thoughts each day our world will change in a special way. Someday soon we will be able to say there's acceptance, peace, and love everywhere and it's here to stay!"

Nalla imagined her heart wings of love traveling all around the world touching people everywhere and helping them see how we are all the same just like Miss Lori said.

Nalla could feel the world was filled with love and her heart was very full.

The end.

A Note to Parents and Educators

This book is designed to help begin conversation in your home or school about acceptance and caring for people everywhere regardless of culture or creed. It is a story about tolerance and kindness. At a deeper level it will support the dream of living in an anti-bias world where we honor all dimensions of human differences.

Wouldn't we all like to see a world where we honor every culture, race, language, ethnicity, religion, gender, age, and more. We need to grow a generation that reaches out and embraces every culture and recognizes the beauty in our differences. I believe this happens when we not only see our differences but embrace the fact that we are all the same in that we are all People. My hope is that this "thoughts are things and love has wings" concept will travel far and wide. I am sure the children will embrace it and hopefully the adult generation will follow in kind.

Please consider teaching your child the heart meditation at the end of this story.

Sending blessings out to all.

Quote by The Dalai Lama:

*"If every 8-year-old in the world is taught meditation,
we will eliminate violence from our world in one generation."*

This is a beautiful quote and idea. However, my thoughts are that all ages can participate in prayer, meditation, mindfulness. Every generation can participate in shifting the mindset of our world. As we teach our children we also learn and shift our own adult paradigm.

So let us begin today...

Heart Meditation for Children

Children love without reservation. Love comes easily to them, and they will enjoy the opportunity to send love out to the world. Please feel free to adapt this according to the age of your child or class. If this is used in school think about it as a "Moment of silence" calling it "heart wing time". Feel free to be creative and use it the way your children will be best served.

1. Sit in a comfortable position and close eyes.

2. Ask children to place both hands on their heart

3. Take a few deep breaths (small children can picture smelling a bouquet of flowers or a delicious pizza)

4. Ask the children to think of someone or something they love very much. (It can be a pet, a person, a place or a favorite memory such as a vacation) Let them sit with this thought and allow it to grow.

5. Now ask them to let the memory go but continue to feel the love in their heart.

6. Now ask them to think of our world. (They can picture a globe/earth, a sky filled with stars, or any other vision that comes to them) Ask them to send all of the love they are feeling in there heart out with heart wings to people everywhere.

7. End by seeing everyone in their picture also loving the world and all this love is coming back to them.

8. Let them sit with this picture for whatever length of time feels right and then thank them all for the heart wings they sent.

For additional information, extension activities for your school or to request the recorded meditation please go to: www.hearwings.us

About the Author

Lori is the mother of four adult daughters Lauren, Katie, Victoria, Kali and a grandmother to Jacob and Gabriella. Born and raised in New Jersey, she lives in Ocean County, New Jersey close to her favorite place...the beach! Her career has included 40+ years as a Child Development Specialist running her own private schools as well as working as a Special Educator for the NJ Early Intervention Program. She has been a lifelong learner earning multiple teaching certifications from Preschool through high school. She holds a MA in Experiential Learning as well as Educational Administration and is currently pursuing her PhD in Nutrition and Natural Health.

About the Illustrator

DC based artist Marques Cannon has been working in various types of art for years including t-shirt design, graphic art, and print illustration. He is a graduate of Ringling College of Art and Design where he originally studied computer animation but later majored in Illustration. Over the years he's cultivated many different styles and is always searching for new ways to evolve and express them.

CPSIA information can be obtained
at www.ICGtesting.com
Printed in the USA
BVHW022138290721
613233BV00014B/280